Praise for *Respirator:*

"*Respirator* is a witch's spellbook or end-time fairy tales, snapshots of dark and beautiful apocalypses seen through the clouded lenses of a gas mask, through the clear and endless portals of interstellar spacecraft. Despite its prophetic here-and-now themes, these stories also carry the nostalgic stamp of classic sci-fi—a little bit of *Solaris* or *Omega Man* subverted with queer identity, strong femininity, and flashes of the surreal. In one later story, a character remarks, 'Death is always a beautiful process because of the way it gives back, but it doesn't always look this blatantly beautiful.' She means a dying star, but she could be describing this collection."

-Brandon Getz, Author, *Lars Breaxface: Werewolf in Space*

"Any time I read an Addison Herron-Wheeler story or poem, I am met with someone who pulls in science fiction, as if creating the perfect pizza, to piece together a beautiful pie of social commentary. Heavy metal spices sprinkled over a sauce of vivid imagery come together to create the beautiful literary entree that is her writing. I highly recommend reading her words in a back corner of Black Sky Brewery with a Brutal Butcher pizza and a nice India Pale Ale. Herron-Wheeler delivers a voice fresh out of the oven."

-Brice Maiurro, Editor-In-Chief, South Broadway Press

"Addison Herron-Wheeler's stylish stories don't pull any punches when it comes to social critique or tech-pessimism, but still hold faint glimmers of redemption and rebellion. *Respirator* hits you with all the speed and fury of a White Lung album."

-Zach Bartlett, Author, *To Another Abyss!*

"*Respirator* is a fantastical journey into a rich and vibrant world that opens as slowly and as beautifully as a flower. It explores thorny issues with a careful and precise distance that allows us to digest the issues raised, yet it is not so far removed that we can't apply the questions each story confronts us with to current times.

"It reminds me of Ray Bradbury's *The Martian Chronicles*. It carries that same expertly maintained distance which allows us to explore sensitive issues without the knee-jerk arguments which so often cripple these topics. At the same time Herron-Wheeler keeps us tethered to current issues through the structure and combination of each story and poem.

"A key example of this is the story *The Weak Whimper of Rape* which explores the wider issues of rape and rape culture by utilizing a futuristic setting and using the plot thread of assassination as a consumer service to push the issue far enough away to observe without being mired by the arguments and counter-arguments so common to the topic of rape culture.

"This book is a journey that is worth every single page turn. It is everything a good science fiction book should be and more."

-Kathy Joy, Author, *Last One To The Bridge*

RESPIRATOR

ADDISON
HERRON-WHEELER

SPACEBOY BOOKS

Denver, Colorado

Published in the United States by:
Spaceboy Books LLC
1627 Vine Street
Denver, CO 80206
www.readspaceboy.com

"Respirator" and "The Ceremony" originally appeared in *Suspect Press*
"Heavy Monsters" originally appeared in *OUT FRONT*
"Virus 08934" originally appeared in *Birdy*
"Drift" originally appeared online at *South Broadway Ghost Society*

First printed May 2020

ISBN: 978-1-951393-02-1

To Wil Wilson and Lexi Holtzer

FOREWORD

I met Addison at a point of growth with my publishing company, Suspect Press. We'd just launched our first book and Addison interviewed my team for a feature in *OUT FRONT* Colorado, complete with an accompanying pagan-themed photoshoot. The first thing I noticed about Addison was her sense of style—her cat-eye glasses and gothic jewelry—and when I learned she was married, polyamorous and bisexual, I knew we were meant to be friends. At the time, I had a dream to teach a weekly writing class, and she encouraged me to follow through with it. This was also a time when I was new to polyamory and exploring my own queer identity, and Addison was kind enough to be my sounding board for all the thoughts and questions I had cycling through my mind.

I'd read her non-fiction work before meeting her, but when she submitted her short fiction story, "Respirator," to *Suspect Press* magazine, I knew immediately it was a story I wanted to publish. I'm excited to see this story now part of a complete collection of Addison's work. The tone of the story, as well as the title, perfectly encapsulate the themes and dystopian world setting of all the stories in this collection. Unpredictably, they also mirror our current times in a chilling, prophetic way—touching on social distancing, mask-wearing, and sanctioned quarantine.

Addison has a knack for immersing readers in an entire alternate universe in very few words. Every story wraps you in a blanket of empathy for each character's state of isolation and guardedness. The world conceived in this collection is not a kind one, but there is kindness tucked inside desperate moments—such as a delivery woman making a snap decision to save a young girl's life despite the risk to her own safety.

Readers are taken through the ravaged streets of Earth as well as on deep space missions where loved ones have been left behind. A particular favorite of mine is the story, "First Mission," in which two top-ranking women take a well-deserved break from their duties to explore the space of each other's bodies. Though not overt, there are multiple hints of queer and open relationships throughout the collection, as though to suggest that monogamy and gender roles are meaningless when the world is ending.

Amidst the character driven stories are a series of softer-themed poems, like odes to the ethereal aspects of life that serve to lift our spirits enough to return and face the unavoidable and necessary darkness. Joy is also found in the savoring of small hangovers from an otherwise forgotten way of life, such as cake, candy, and canned peaches.

I'm excited to see these stories enter the world after seeing many of them in their early stages, several of which were incubated in the very writing class Addison inspired me to host. May you find them sincere in their emotional relatability and may you be entertained by each surreal adventure.

Amanda E.K., Editor-in-chief, Suspect Press[1]

---

[1] Suspect Press is an awesome Denver-based publishing company. They aren't affiliated with Spaceboy Books, LLC., but you should look them up online at suspectpress.com. – *ed.*

TABLE OF CONTENTS

RESPIRATOR

Neeka pulled on her gas mask and headed out into the smoggy street. Looking around, she noticed everyone on the street was wearing some kind of face protection. Although she only had to walk five blocks between her day job filing papers and her night shift as an exotic dancer, she didn't want to risk breathing the toxic air. Her mask was old, picked up from a local shelter, and her breath came in short little gasps as she walked.

She paused before the solid steel door to The Tower, the night club where she worked. Pulling her mask down, she glanced around before heading inside. She could technically lose her day job for working at a place like this by night. Her salvation was that she donned her gas mask during her act, along with bondage gear and tight black latex. The irony of her ode to the fetishization of the apocalypse was lost on the mindless drones that sipped plasmid mixers until their eyes were glazed and shoved dollars into the jar on stage.

Neeka pulled her mask back up as soon as she got inside, even though her eyes had to work double-time to adjust to the darkness of the club after the blinding afternoon sun. She made her way by sheer instinct to the backstage area and tossed her bag onto a grimy bench in front of a cracked mirror. She was ready for her show in less than five minutes; after pulling off her dress and leggings to reveal her latex getup, she simply readjusted her mask and teased up her hair.

From the stage, she could tell that it was going to be a busy night. A group of young executives were gathered at a table right near her platform, celebrating with a round of plasmids. It seems that they closed a deal that day and were now taking each other out. She actually recognized them from her floor in the Energy Center where she filed papers and answered phones, but she preferred to think about that as little as possible. Although it was very unlikely anyone would recognize her with the mask on, or in this outfit compared with the modest and even puritanical dresses she wore to the office, they could easily ask her supervisor, and for a little bit of extra cash, discover her identity. Neeka knew that even though she was one of the best dancers, she could expect no real loyalty from either of her places of employment.

One of the men approached the stage, egged on by his friend, standing right behind him and making comments about Neeka's body. She tried to ignore them and continued her dance. For the most part, people respected the no-touching policy and put money in the jar, or were just at the club for its subversive appeal and ignored the dancers altogether. Since strip clubs were technically considered prostitution and ruled illegal, many simply wanted to experience nostalgia or some cheap thrill by visiting the dive.

The same man got closer, and his friend nudged him and muttered something in his ear. He reached up, and at first Neeka thought he was going to put some money in her jar. Then his hand jutted past the jar, up onto the stage, and grabbed her crotch hard, bringing her to her knees.

Something inside Neeka snapped, and before she realized what she was doing, she pulled out the knife she kept on her leg for walking home after her shifts and jabbed it directly into the man's stomach, thrusting upward. She watched as though seeing a scene from a film as he staggered forward, blood gushing from the wound on his stomach. His friend yelled something derogatory and threw a bottle. Blood continued to spurt. A woman at a nearby table let out a shrill scream, and the repetitive, bass-driven music abruptly stopped. Without hesitation, Neeka leapt from the stage and ran for the door and out onto the street.

A thousand thoughts pounded through her mind as she ran. Of course, her phone and wallet were inside, and her employers would be calling the police giving a full description of who she was. It was over—she couldn't go back to work, and she would be hunted day-in and out by the drones constantly hovering over the city. She ran and ran without stopping, going at least 15 blocks before she dropped to her knees, gasping for air, unable to take another step.

Suddenly, out of the fog, she heard a lilting melody.

This land is your land; this land is my land..

The voices got closer, and soon she could make out a group of hooded figures dressed in white. A fleet of priestesses were out on their nightly walk, singing softly. In-between verses, they all puffed on the respirators they carried with them, making the song sound more dirgelike than Neeka imagined it was meant to.

The women were all around her now, encircling her. For a moment she panicked; she had no idea what these women actually did or whether they would turn her in or attack her. She was covered in blood, dressed in a bondage outfit with a gas mask on. She waited for them to say something. Anything. Then she noticed that one of the priestesses was holding a robe out to her. Neeka suddenly understood that probably the only way she could hide is if she pretended to be one of them. She pulled on the robe and took off her mask, tossing it aside onto the street. Inside the robe was a respirator like the ones the women used. Slowly, she fell into step with them as they made their way down the block singing their woeful song.

This land was made for you and me...

BURNT EMBERS

She went outside every chance she got, between the warning sirens, and whenever dawn broke clear through the graying atmosphere.

She occasionally took her gas mask off and breathed the air for as long as she could before she had to put it back on. Sometimes, she saw particles dancing against the ashen skyline like faeries flitting home before night descended.

She knew, absolutely knew, that no one was coming for her, that no one would find her in that spot. She stored old rain water in bottles and drank only the ones that passed the Ph tests. Rain came often, but sometimes, it was more acid than rain, and it was necessary to take shelter inside the decrepit factory for days.

She knew that going up on the roof was risky, but the view was breathtaking. Even though half the skyline had been destroyed and there were always patches of smoke, some fire, she enjoyed looking out at what once had been. And even though the lights she saw at night were from fires and not electricity, she still loved the magical glint of the city.

She didn't have anyone to talk to, so she invented friends, characters, drew them on the walls, had lunch with them. She wrote poems on her walls and colored in an entire mural of the skyline. She counted the days by drawing hearts on a space near where she slept. None of this made her crazy; she would have gone crazy without some way to pass the time.

She imagined sometimes that the city was actually being reclaimed by the faeries and sprites she had played with as a girl. She used to think that they lived in the quiet spaces in the park where there was no trash, that they wrote her letters in perfect gold script on light pink paper that crinkled in the wind. She pretended that more of them were coming out now that less humans were around. She pretended they could breathe the radioactive air, that they were actually made of radioactive particles.

She remembered reading in school that radioactive particles were actually found in space, that they occurred naturally in things like comets. So she imagined that faeries were from space, that they rode down on comets and meteors and found safety in the radioactive city. They were actually in their elements here. Their wings were made of cosmic dust and they breathed out radioactive comet trails. They dreamed of moonbeams and someday flying back home to their very own planets, which maybe had been made uninhabitable because of too many non-radioactive particles entering the atmosphere.

She did yoga to strengthen her breathing in the gas mask, stay in shape and not go crazy. Her yoga mat was a cardboard box that she flattened out and stuck to the floor. She ran through the poses she remembered from the days of the internet and from the few classes she had taken.

She ate a lot of cake that was pilfered from a local grocery store. She had read somewhere that cake was one of those foods you could eat even after an apocalyptic event because it wasn't easily contaminated. Or, maybe it was that it was easily contaminated because it was like a sponge, and she was actually just eating cake because she was lonely and bored and wasn't sure where she would get cake again once she had exhausted this supply.

She didn't expect to see anyone in the city, but was ready for what would happen if she did. She felt she had to be prepared for anything, but she didn't really have weapons except for a stick she had sharpened. She entertained fantasies sometimes about meeting up with a group and leaving, and she had nightmares about being discovered by someone she couldn't fight back against. But the days went by, and nothing.

She went up onto the roof one evening to take a look at the dying skyline, to watch the fires slowly glint into being. This had to mean there were more people, unless her faeries were real, or unless there were fires out there that hadn't been put out somehow.

She saw movement behind the factory building directly across from her. A glint of bright blonde, it looked like. She blinked, peering into the night, trying to see as the light grew dimmer. She saw another flicker, and then what was unmistakably a foot.

She watched as a figure stepped out from behind the building. It was a faerie. She had long blond dreadlocks, was dressed all in brown. Her shoes seemed to be made out of plastic bags, and she was carrying what looked like a sharpened stick as well. Her face was a gas mask, until the mask was lifted and she looked up.

She knew it might have been foolish, but she started jumping up and down, waving, smiling, yelling that she had a bit of cake inside, some water, and that she had been alone for months. Of course, she was taking a chance with the faerie. And if the faerie came inside, the faerie would be taking a chance with her.

She stopped and looked down, terrified that the faerie would run. They both met each others' gaze for a moment, sized each other up, and she smiled.

The faerie smiled.

SILVER WHITE

It was long after dark, and I knew better than to walk the streets alone. I felt the fear rising from the pavement, could almost sense it before I looked out the window and saw the gang gathered in the street below. I pulled my worn shawl more tightly around my shoulders and glanced down, wincing.

I didn't really fear them seeing me—there were at least 20 people sleeping downstairs. It's not that they would protect me—I was another stranger to them; they didn't know me—but they would make it impossible for me to be targeted. I had done it many nights before— laid face-down, rags covering me, hunched up as much as I could. I found that if I hid my figure almost completely that way, the gangs would pass me over, just search our stuff for loot, and be out of my way.

So it is still not clear to me what drove me out of the abandoned shack down on 38th Street that evening. I was on the far edge of town – although I could still see what remained of the smoldering city skyline. This neighborhood was once considered bad, or low-income, or non-white, and was separated from the rest of the city by what used to be the interstate, and the train tracks.

This now provided an advantage, as the heart of the city was where the most rapes, murders, and constant looting occurred. Out here on the edges, one could hide out with some cans of food and buy a little time in a room, surrounded by strangers doing the same thing.

Gangs must have figured there was less food, fewer things to seize, in what used to be the poor neighborhoods.

Still, when we were bound up in a house like this, to hold off the night and stave off those who sought to do us harm, there was no sense of camaraderie. It was not cozy—there were no lights on because we feared drawing attention to ourselves, and there was no sharing of goods, because we feared not having enough for ourselves, or maybe that someone in the house was secretly a looter, just someone between gangs, or looking to rest up for a few nights before going back out on the streets. The few people who were together tried to share food and goods carefully, and hide any signs of affection or companionship, as though these signs of weakness proved they had more to lose.

But I was lucky—I didn't have anyone to worry about, to look over my shoulder for, to fear for. I had at one time, but they were already gone, and as each day went by, I began to see that as less and less of a burden and more of a blessing.

I remembered some TV shows or books or movies about post-apocalyptic scenarios I had seen or read a few years before. No matter how dark these stories were, people banded together—they found each other, clung to each other, formed new social groups that inevitably forced them into remembering what it was to be social—then they had new things to lose, and the story arc could continue, an array of sadness. But real humans don't work that way—it is as though we know that the switch for those kinds of connections needs to be turned off. Those relationships, if they do still exist, need to be muted, and new bonds aren't being formed. The only bonds forming are between those who choose to pillage and rape and rampage instead of hide out in the dark, and those are also superficial.

That night I can't say why I chose to venture out, and so far into the city, down the footpath into the heart of town. Yes, I was hungry— of course, we were all hungry, and yes, I was starting to feel that inevitable doom that is hopelessness, that is *not* caring at all or fearing for my life, but it was more than that. It was an old feeling, one that I thought we surely must have done away with in these times, but hadn't—boredom.

I simply needed to move, to breathe, to walk through what was once the city even if it was now smoldering. I could have easily sought food or cans or sustenance in a nearby crash house that was now abandoned, or an old restaurant or convenience store in my neighborhood. It would have even been dangerous—someone could have been sleeping, or lurking, or waiting anywhere—but it wasn't a death-wish, thrill-seeking kind of boredom. It was the kind that used to strike me on summer days as a child—the desire to get out, and see, and do.

I silently crept away from the window as soon as the gang had passed, stepping over sleeping bodies. A few jerked upward, aggressively, something I had become accustomed to because of the way everyone was always on edge. I murmured an apology and held my head down, enough for them to learn I wasn't a threat, wasn't doing any harm, and continued on down the stairs.

At the very foot of the stairs lay a man, his eyes open, staring glassily at me as I passed. His face seemed to light up when I got closer, seeing my figure and my dirty face. This too was familiar—while passable as another refugee by day, with no desire to loot or pillage, he dealt with his losses at night with too much drink, which could cause him to be dangerous. Quickly I doubled over and coughed loudly, pretending to be sick and have a sudden fit, covering my mouth.

A few others sat up or rolled over. While I knew they wouldn't protect me out of care for me, anyone who wanted to cause harm was remotely a threat to all, and a sick woman who was coughing blood wasn't a good target for him. The man shifted, closed his eyes, and appeared to slump against the wall. I moved quickly through the hallway by the door, and out into the street.

I glanced over my shoulder a few times to make sure the man wasn't following me, then darted into a nearby alley to be sure. I had charged my phone recently, as the house I had stayed in the night before still had electricity, and I pulled it out now and used my flashlight to shine around in the dark and make sure no new threats lurked. When I had waited a few minutes and was satisfied that the man had already forgotten me, had rolled over and gone back to sleep, I slipped out onto the street and began to walk quickly.

I made my way through the alleys and streets to the footbridge without incident. I knew this neighborhood so well by now that I knew all the trouble spots, anywhere gangs did hang out when they came this far, and where to hide if I saw them.

At one point I darted into an alley to avoid approaching voices, only to discover it was a man who was sick, accompanied by a woman who was crying, trying to convince him it was something else besides what they both knew it was. I didn't allow myself to think about what they would both face in the morning. I closed my eyes and for a brief moment pretended they were walking home from the bar, drunk, laughing, ready to fall asleep in each other's arms, or even just fighting—the man had had too much to drink and started a fight, the woman had become too friendly with a stranger. I darted back onto the street and made it to the bridge.

Once in the city, things were different. I could smell the ash here so strongly that I almost gagged. There seemed to be something wrong with the air in the city besides the ash. It felt thick and hot, almost like something other than oxygen, and I wondered, not for the first time, if some kind of chemical had at some point been spread to counter the sickness. The tall building I had always admired with the shining, color-changing steeple was knocked askew, and now only coldly reflected the light of the full moon, a blinding silver-white.

Until now, I had not really thought of where to go—I just wanted to walk, to be out. It now occurred to me that if I moved to the part of town that used to be an outdoor mall, I may be able to find some remaining food. I knew that gang activity used to be so heavy there it was impossible to walk even during the daytime, but I also knew from whispered reports and talks with strangers that the gangs had now mostly moved to the southern side of the city, and to the suburbs, which probably held more food.

As I crept out onto the cobblestone, I heard voices, and darted into the nearby alley. I had no idea what this alley held, but before I could shine my phone and get some light, I heard what was unmistakably a gang, this time outside.

"There's nothing here man, nothing—unless we can score some kind of action soon. I'm gonna head east and look for some liquor."

I heard a smashed bottle and a screaming laugh, and knew that if I were to be discovered this was even worse—a bored group with nothing to do would surely take advantage of me, knowing there were no other worthy distractions in the area. Just then, I heard a voice behind me.

"Hey, what're you doing this side of town so late—your husband go ill on you?"

It couldn't be, but it was—the same glass-eyed drunk man from the house had followed me here. Or he hadn't ever followed me, but there was one of them on every corner, or in every alley. And he had once been a business man, or a father, or he had always been homeless and lived on these streets, and he had once been somebody's son, or crush, or maybe husband. Now he just got up and walked closer to me, swinging a bottle.

And I thought I fainted, although I couldn't have, because I remember clearly what happened next. The street turned a blinding white, and I couldn't see in front of me or beside me. My mind raced—another attack, army helicopters after all, someone coming to the rescue, or else some awful trick, some toy of the gang or group's that they planned to use to trap me.

When the light subsided, I saw a shining, towering, silver-white horse standing in the square in front of me. It was exceedingly tall—it seemed to me to be as tall as the ruined buildings, to reach the moon itself, yet I could see the top of it. It was a naked woman on a horse, but at the same time it wasn't—it was a woman and a horse at the same time. It made a sound that shrieked and shrilled and moaned. It was as if it was taking the whole city down with it, wrapping it up in its sound, destroying everything with its breath. It was as though the city froze and turned white as ash. It was the sound of an air raid and also a lovely singing—both kind of siren.

I tried to look ahead of me, but everything was that blinding white color. My ears rang, and I looked wildly around, fearing what could come upon me during the attack. Then I saw clearly in front of me, a figure walking right towards me. It was not man or beast, or woman for that matter. It had lost all sense of being a horse, or a maiden on a horse, whatever I had thought before.

It was now simply a sexless, genderless, towering figure. It seemed to reach out a hand, and when it did, a great blackness cut into the blinding white. I saw little traces of red running away from the black of the hand, breaking up the white. I heard a cold breathing, almost as if someone were whispering right by my ear. I began to scream with all my might—a scream that unleashed all the pain and fear and quiet I had been holding in for the past few months. I screamed until I couldn't even feel my voice anymore, and I knew I had exhausted it. My knees buckled, and I fell to the ground.

When I awoke, everything was colder, and quieter. My ears were ringing, and I felt them; they were bleeding. Other than that, things seemed to be the same, but there was no sign of the man from the alley or the gang from the street. I looked around me, and walked, glancing nervously over my shoulder for a long time, in case they appeared. Then I walked back to the edge of town to cross the bridge.

SPACE RITUAL

astral bodies
cold space/ blackened witches/ dark wings spread open
space ritual
astral bodies

rebirth in the stars—
a cosmic lullaby

****

Can you hear them whispering?
Long ago they were us—the astral bodies

∞

A nebula is not something that forgives
A ghost planet—a lost world
thousands of astral bodies, displaced
"we are all made of stars" whispered your alien mother on a faraway
planet before she had to send you on an asteroid, drifting, on a comet,
pummeling through the atmosphere of earth, on fire, a million miles
an hour, and at least a million degrees.

Space Ritual
make this a safe space for all alien transgressors, all helpless witches
burned at the asteroid stake
crucified for understanding the location of the stars in the sky
or made into a god, an astral body
or simply sentenced to become one with the stars
a cosmic death
does suffocation in space feel like drowning? Can it feel like drowning
when there is no way to fight up, for air?

****

We are made from the same stuff as stars, the man on TV told me, as
the picture blurred in and out, the lines curved
what a nice pattern, a nice design, to have nebulas adorn your body,
to end the life of a star with every slight movement, shimmer

Expanding out
and possibly there is nothing, truly
but these astral bodies that keep time
with the rhythm of the universe
you say, it's all one,
but you say it with sarcasm
because our bodies can't yet dissolve into the stars

you tell me to create a safe space, for an open dialogue
I keep screaming inwardly, space is not safe
not for the astral bodies that only live a few billion years
then explode
so rudely, and almost effortlessly

I have once perched on the moon, my witch
you tell me so confidently that I forget about your alien skin for a
moment
and that you don't mean this moon
but Titan, and you don't mean now
but a million years in the future, when I am dead

we're all sprinkles
you whisper
from the same cosmic watering can
astral to astral, dust to dust

rebirth in the stars –
a cosmic lullaby

****

Can you hear them whispering?
Long ago they were us—the astral bodies

∞

BLUES FROM THE CORE

Going inside Pluto's inner core
That astral plane
That void nothingness
Like a cozy outcropping
On the edge of oblivion
Forever, for never, no
Moons orbit it
That astral blackness
So unsure of its own existence
And devoid of its own forgiveness

I'd like to dive into
The depths of Europa
And gaze on Saturn in all its glory
I'll twine myself in the
Tentacles of the
Primordial ooze
That gives life below
The cracked ice
In yellow and green hues

I want to dissolve my body
In the astral bodies of the universe

And heal the sick & dying stars on TV
And the stars that blink out
Far off
Dying red & pale & ghostly

I want to embody the very essence
Of what it is to be a super nova
I want Carl Sagan's ghost
To peer out of that
Psychonotic astral travelling
Machine and say

—My what a beauty—
As he adjusts his
Synesthesia-word turtleneck
Of purple protest

I want a thousand starry-eyed dreamers outside of Kansas
With thick calves and
Bad tattoos to feel compelled
To play music at 10000 MPH b/c of my
Slow fade into nothingness
My twinkle

I want to burn at the stake
Of 1000 gas giants
For telling a king
That the earth is round

Or maybe to be
Crucified upside down
At the creation museum
B/c I wore a tanktop to school

But mostly I just
Want to burn burst &
Catch flame

Like that Johnny Rotten/Sex Pistol
Explosion of good faith

No slow doom drone fade
No astral projection

INVASION OF THE BODY SNATCHERS

MEDITATIONS ON THE X-FILES

Mulder, have you heard about the corpses?
All baby bodies laid at in a row
Each taken from a different mother
And some not human??

Mulder, have you stayed awake long enough to hear them pull out
your eyeballs
And dump black sludge down your throat
And tear off your limbs
And kill my baby?

Mulder, do you know why it is you could never make love to me?
Am I your sister?
Are you saving our vessels, our wombs, our very souls
For the invaders you are waiting for?

Mulder, they gave me cancer
Because I am the cancer
The smoking man blew me a shotgun and laughed into space

His eyes were gone, only black sludge remained

Mulder, my sister was taken too
Were they both stabbed in the throat with a thin pin,
Were they filled with the future of mankind
Did they give birth to black sludge as they gazed up at the skylight?

Mulder, I can't understand what it is they want with me
Someone is objectifying my red hair
Someone is breathing into my throat
Someone is calling me mother

Mulder, I loved you once,
Now I lay on this table and watch for my baby
A swollen belly, soft lighting,
You noticed in the next season I lost weight
You laughed a coy laugh about our little secret while we waited for
the sea monster
Did you know they took my child?

STAR HAIR

Cascading, blue and purple
Like milk, like rain

Flowing onto the comforter covered in stars, blue and silent in the
soft red light

Blue with flecks of perfect gold and stardust
Closed eyes, freckles like stars
Melting over the highway

Cascading like waves
Dripping out of space

DRAGON GALAXY

Glazed eyes traced in stardust, ringed with fear
The dragon lurks behind the clouds
Some astral spiral arm galaxy away, floating beneath swords

The dragon approaches, folding wings, enfolding planets in its stare
A star supernovas in its wake, fearful of the space wind he rides
Purple poison seeps from his mouth

**//
BURN/BURST
//**

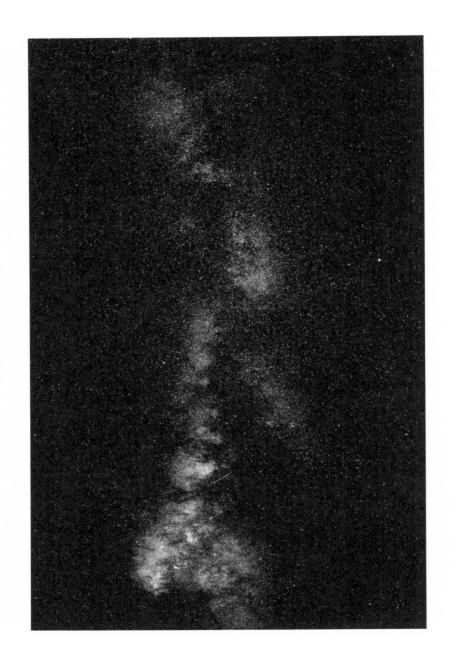

BLOSSOMING DEATH

She woke thousands of years from her birth, but in a familiar place. At first all she could see was the green glow of the tube she was encased in. As she was released from it, the red light poured in, doubling her over in pain. Then the memories slowly came.

Panic, fear, the constant sense that something was wrong. Looking over her shoulder, hearing whispered talk about a bomb, a future of pain and sorrow. And then it came, the crash, so full of color. Reds and golds exploded in an unfolding, sensual mushroom cloud she watched burst. When it happened, it was like a dream. She saw it, and at first couldn't process what really happened.

Then, constant running, staying on the move. Always looking for the next place to sleep, foraging for food, wearing masks, feeling the radiation sickness infect her more and more each day. Until she had found them, a colony of people running and hiding like her, with the science to heal her sickness, the tools to make her well again.

Finally, calm days stretched before her like a warm blanket. She may be hiding, underground and crowded, but there was consistent food, regular showers, a bed, even human connection. It was more like the life she missed.

Then came dissent. One of her fellow survivors, a particular man, was adamant that the women should be used for breeding in order to continue the human race. The days of comfort turned to fear, and she felt she'd be better off out on the open road again. She was kept in a room, fed, and ritually raped. She gave birth several times without anesthesia to children she never saw again.

But even that horror ended. When the overcrowding became too much, it was decided that the most fertile women should be frozen in case of mutations or another natural disaster. At that point, her spirit was so broken from the rape and the constant pregnancy and childbirth that she willingly went into the tube.

As she was put under, a series of pictures and colors flashed before her eyes. The bomb exploding over and over, and blooming into a gorgeous flower. She coughed and choked on an imaginary smell of sulphur behind her eyes as cryogenic freezing began to take hold of her senses. The next thing she smelled were the fetid juices of the vat sloshing as she fell forward into the new world.

The sensations of this new state of being were too much for her, and she collapsed onto her knees, blacking out.

When she came to, she was in a soft, comfortable bed with music playing and flowers all around her. Their colors softly bloomed before her as she once again got used to vision. The white, sliding door to her room glided open, and a figure stepped in.

"You're awake. I still can't believe you're really here."

The person who stood before her was tall and slender with blue-grey skin and soft features. They had no hair, but beautiful green eyes, and appeared to be neither male, nor female. While the person didn't look like anyone she had ever seen, she felt comforted instead of scared.

"You've been asleep for a long time," the figure said kindly. "It's been what you would have counted as 2,479 years. The cryogenic freezing techniques of your time were extremely archaic, so you have aged about five years during the process, and you unfortunately may have some lingering side effects to your senses of smell and hearing. But, somehow, a few of you dimorphics actually managed to survive."

"Dimorphics? You mean... no one else looks like me?"

"No one but other survivors. Thousands of years ago, as your people hid from radiation underground, the world above died and was destroyed. The ancient dimorphics forced procreation on female-bodied people in order for the race to survive. We can only assume that's what happened to you. Finally, a group of dimorphics got fed up with the rape and horror and overthrew the ones in charge. They focused on how to procreate artificially, because not only did they want to do away with the pain and suffering of forced procreation, they also wanted to weed out the mutations that were still seeping through."

"So," they continued, "Eventually, they perfected a race of people who are not sexually dimorphic, hence our name for your ancient kind."

As she was listening to the speech, she looked over at one of the flowers on the bed next to her. It seemed to be opening up before her eyes, the beautiful light pinks and bright reds expanding just like the clouds of death she had witnessed so many centuries ago.

"I understand this may be a shock to you, and we welcome you to stay here and take your time adjusting to it as long as you need," they said. "When you're ready, you can join our society, meet others like you who have survived, and also others like me."

"Where is *here*?" She asked. Suddenly visions of an underground city full of grey buildings and people, a foreign planet, flashed through her mind, and for the first time, she felt scared.

They gently bent over her, smiling reassuringly, and pulled back the curtain beside the bed. Outside, rows and rows of flowers bloomed in all colors. There were more colors and plants than she had ever seen. They all blended into each other.

"This is one of our biggest indoor nature preserves. We call it The Garden, and we house cryogenic survivors in it because of the comforting effects of the plants. When you feel up to it, would you like to go out and have a look around?"

For the first time, she smiled.

"Yes. I'd like to do that now, and I think I'd like to stay here for a while."

BLOOD AND TEETH

Nothing was changed outside. The world was exactly as it was before. No one had even noticed that she was slowly wasting away, closer than ever to the end. And no one had noticed that the two women had been living in complete isolation for the last 37 years, although in the past, they had occasionally ventured out to gather supplies.

Now they had everything they needed. Thankfully, they were used to hiding and then resurfacing years later. When you lived for hundreds of years, it started to draw suspicion. Witches never thought very far ahead, or at least never seemed to.

She and her sister had looked 89 or 90 for about 500 years now, and that was the rough part. Centuries of childhood were a breeze; centuries of teen years and young adulthood were a gift from the ancient ones. It occurred to her that maybe other witches killed themselves years before they reached this point.

Just that morning, when she was looking into the reflective hologram, her tongue had fallen out, blood pouring out into the ether. Her lips were already gone, and before that, her ears. There was almost nothing left. Thousands of years ago, there had been breathless kisses in a dark movie theater, moans beneath the sheets, food and drinks and laughter.

Now she stood and looked out at a world of machines, holding her sister in her hands. They were all around her. They had assimilated all human life. To her, this wasn't a positive or a negative, merely a fact. She and her sister didn't register as human life, or for that matter, as life at all, so they were allowed to continue on.

Lovers had already wasted away, years ago, dying a slow, happy death, or later a quick, painful one. She opened her toothless, tongueless, lipless mouth and gave one last low, horrible moan. The last of the human race had long passed. Here was the last of the witches.

As she screamed, green, rotted slime poured forth from her lips and slowly engulfed her and her sister, turning them into ooze. All was quiet, and the stars blinked up above.

VEGETABLE GARDEN

Rotting Plums stealing away the soul from
What was once a place for raspberries

Dead, gutted weeds and ferns choke out all signs of life

If you lie still beneath the soil
You can hear the strangled cry of a dying infant left in the sun too
long
Now hungry to dry and left to rot

Peeled, already chewed
Regurgitated potatoes and carrots line the rotted earth

Sinking into the fetid soil full of blood and despair

Soon my garden will grow again
Full of rot and disease
Ripe for the picking

BLUE GLOW

Kalta rolled over and grabbed her phone from the floor beside her rolled sleeping bag. Rubbing her eyes, she hit the Friend Finder icon and began to scroll through the news feed.

"Thank goodness the quarantine patrols have passed me by. #safefornow."

"Five patrols seen walking down 4th and Elwood. Steer clear."

"Another explosion off of 13th in the north side of town. Major air contamination. #maskup."

Kalta sighed and rifled around in her bag for her mask. She had been banking on the north side of town staying relatively safe, but it appeared that the Invaders had made it further into the city than she had anticipated.

She took one more glance at her phone through the blurry lens of the mask before darkening her screen.

"43rd on the west side remains relatively free of patrol parties and Invaders. #staysafe."

Although she had no desire to see or meet up with anyone she was connected to online, Kalta was running out of options when it came to survival. Three quarters of the city were pretty much off limits, and she could already hear distant gunfire outside, proof that remaining Resisters were putting up a fight against an incoming threat.

Kalta didn't know what would actually be worse, getting caught by a quarantine patrol or getting blasted by Invaders. Dying slowly of radiation poisoning sounded awful, and worse, it was said that some of the Invaders took prisoners to their ship. The quarantine patrols claimed that they took in survivors and helped them, kept them safe, even relocated them to sanctioned camps that were protected by the Army. Enough photos and testimony from those taken had now leaked out on social media, however, that it was clear this was not the case. In reality, anyone who had been "exposed" to radiation in the city for too long was euthanized because they posed too big of an infection risk.

Still, being killed quickly by some kind of injection seemed better than being taken to an alien spaceship and dissected. Of course, there were all kinds of rumors about the Invaders, but no one was really sure why they had shown up to Earth and started to wage war.

Kalta shuddered and pulled her sleeping bag up around her shoulders, savoring that last bit of warmth and comfort before she had to venture out into the night. She didn't want anything probing her mind or pulling her body apart while she was still alive. And now her only connection to the rest of the world, and the only clue she had for where to go or what to do, was the stupid app on her phone that everyone used to share information.

She had completely detested social media before the collapse of everything. It made her sick to have to sort through overly entitled opinions and pictures of peoples' stupid families and pets. Worse was that everyone else seemed to love it and buy into it when she detested it. She had even got in a fight with her ex-boyfriend when she refused to make any kind of profile and share the fact that they were in a relationship. Now she had a profile, but she didn't share any photos or posts, and never, ever shared any tips about her location or how to stay safe. There was too much risk of someone out there coming to take advantage of her.

It was time to move. Kalta stood up and slowly rolled her sleeping bag, shuddering in the cold of the abandoned room. She reached into her pack to get an extra pair of socks, two sweaters, a hat and a scarf. She then pulled on her combat boots and giant parka. Whatever the Invaders were bombing the city with was making it unbearably cold. Grabbing her pack and shoving her phone in her pocket, Kalta started down the stairs.

She walked uninterrupted for the first few blocks, with just the echoes of explosions and screams behind her. Once she reached 20th, she sat down on the bench to wait for the bus. One of the oddest things about everything that had happened in the past months was that most of the systems and institutions she had come to expect were still running as usual. It was still possible to catch a bus most of the time. If a bus was blown up and a driver was killed, they would just put another bus and another driver on the route the next day.

The bus took its time winding through the streets; a few times it had to detour and go another way because too many bodies or too much debris from an explosion were blocking the road. Finally, Kalta arrived at 38th street. The mechanical voice warned her about securing strollers and all belongings before boarding.

Her plan was to make it to the area around 43rd and find a place to hole up, but as soon as she got to the corner of 42nd, she sensed something was wrong. She heard a loud hissing that drowned out the distant echoes of the warzone further downtown.

Turning the corner onto 43rd, Kalta was stopped in her tracks by an Invader standing in her way. She had never seen the grotesque, twisting muscles on the giant's decaying face so close up before. The only way she could really describe the Invaders was that they looked like huge, decomposing people. The smell of rotten eggs was unbearable, and she heard a heavy, labored breathing.

The Invader reached up and began to tug on the rotting flesh of its face. As Kalta watched in horror, it pulled off what appeared to be a mask. Shiny blond hair hung down, and blue eyes flashed from the face of a young, beautiful woman. She reached in her pocket and held out a phone to Kalta.

"Just in time," she said, smiling sweetly. "I thought you'd never come."

THE WEAK WHIMPER
OF RAPE[1]

She really didn't know if it was worth it to kill, but she wanted to find out. There were two ways she could go about it. One, the most popular way, was to simply tap the icon and someone, somewhere, in the world, would die. She would never know whom or how. By that token, it was really more of a thing to do to feel powerful, to have some sense of control.

And the other was to kill a specific person.

Mari was different in that she had no desire to kill her rapists. True, multiple men had had their turns with her, each more brutal than the last. But in that sense, they were really all the same. Should she choose the one who started it or the one who was most brutal?

Also, strangely, she would never be able to identify the men, even using face recognition tools of the most advanced kind. In her mind, it was all a blur. She had heard this could happen after trauma. Literally any man walking down the street could be her rapist. Only little boys were out.

But another face she remembered all-too-well. It was the face of the woman who had stumbled on her being raped and not done anything. She remembered looking over and even making eye contact

---

[1] a reference to Harlan Ellison's "The Whimper of Whipped Dogs" and Fritz Leiber's "Smoke Ghost.

with her as she passed by the alley. Her hair was long, straight, and dark, and her eyes flashed a vivid green. She was gaunt and slim with a wide face.

Their eyes had locked. Mari's must have been pleading for help. She must have been screaming. What got her was the look. It was a long, hard look as though the woman were memorizing every detail of the scene. Then, she slowly turned and walked away. The woman didn't run. She didn't get scared. Cowardice, Mari could have forgiven her. After all, what was stopping the men from grabbing her, too?

No, it was the concentrated, studying look, the eye contact, and the slow walking away. Sometimes, Mari doubted her own memory. If this had really happened, why hadn't the men grabbed her too? How could it have been that she so cooly observed and then walked away?

But Mari knew what she had seen. This is why she would kill the woman who had simply watched. She made up her mind to do it one day when she was washing dishes and thinking. She was picturing the woman's unforgiving eyes for the millionth time, and something within her snapped.

The next day, she took all her money out of the private savings account she kept hidden from her husband. She had more than enough to treat herself to a lavish shopping spree, make some solid investments, or start her own life. But *this* was more important.

This was revenge.

She arrived at the room; a simple, white door with a blue doorbell. As she had been instructed, she rang the doorbell three times, waited, and then rang it four times. Approximately five minutes later, the door seemed to swing open on its own. Uncertainly, Mari walked in.

She walked down a long hall and into a room, where she sat across from a beautiful woman in a simple, white coat. While classically gorgeous, the woman wasn't wearing any makeup or jewelry, and her hair was down in wisps around her face.

Working together and using facial recognition technology, Mari explained in great, painstaking detail every feature of the staring woman's face. Soon, like a ghost coming back from the dead, the woman's face appeared on the screen before her.

The woman in white frowned and then scrunched up her face.

"Is this some kind of joke?"

Mari felt as though she had been slapped in the face.

"No, this is definitely not a joke. This woman watched me get raped as though she were watching a training video, or looking in passing at a painting. Then she walked away like she was leaving the grocery store. No fear, no panic, and no sympathy. She is a monster."

"This is the famous actress Wila Douglas," the woman replied. "I can't believe you haven't seen her."

Mari rarely watched TV and didn't care about celebrities.

"No, I've never seen her."

The woman then proceeded to bring up more pictures of the woman with her family, with her husband and child, on the set of a movie.

"Her most famous film is *Desperate for Desire.*"

She pulled up a new screen, this time showing the woman forced into an alley way, with multiple men being forced on her. The fear in the woman's eyes, and her desperate screams, were the exact same as Mari's. She was channeling her exact emotions.

Mari reached across the table and swiped at the screen in front of the woman. The woman jumped back a little, then tried to regain her composure and settle into her chair.

"You realize, of course, that a celebrity is triple the fee."

"Yes, I realize that. I have more than enough; it won't be a problem."

Slowly, the woman in white reached across the table with a special red tablet and rolled back its cover. On its screen was a single app, with a circle labelled *Press Here.* Mari breathed hard, looked at the screen, and then stabbed at the circle with his index finger.

RESPIRATOR II

Neeka was living with the sisters in the mountains, wrapped in red cloth to tell her apart from the numbers. She was a guest in their sanctuary. She didn't belong there, but they let her walk among them.

She felt the cool wind pour into her chamber one day, and she knew it was time to leave. Mercy, they had shown her mercy when reality became too much. When she stabbed a man, bathed in his blood as she was draped in red now, and she hadn't regretted it.

They sang their hymns of Old America, before the plagues came, before everything changed. They circled each other, breathed in white light, mercury. Now she knew she had to leave their comfort and keep running.

They would eventually look for her here. She had to keep going, even though she didn't know where. She cast off her red robe. There was no mirror in her quarters, but she looked down and saw she had grown bony. She pulled on the stained, white dress they had given her as a slip, and tied back her hair.

Out in the corridor, she could hear echoes like music coming from all directions. It was the sound of the sisters doing their separate devotionals, all blending together. The sounds followed her as she headed down the long, marble hallway, slinking past the closed doors.

Once she had made it to the courtyard, Neeka could breathe again. All she had was the few dollars she had hidden away in her underwear, her light cotton dress. She headed in the direction of the rubble, the city. She followed the smoke and smog rising against the sunset.

HEAVY MONSTERS

During our first years inside, we used to run through the halls, jumping over pipes and dancing in the hissing steam. We would hide behind the old machinery, ready to jump out at each other and scream, shrieking through the halls. With everything going on outside, I don't know why we craved the rush, but we did. Sleeping all day to avoid the poisonous gas outside made us restless.

We used to steal candy along with canned goods when we went out with our gas masks, raiding the stores. It was sealed, so it was safe to eat, and we also loved the way it made us feel, the tingling sensation in our temples as we chased each other around.

It must have been October when the bombs first fell, because the stores were also full of costumes. We needed clothes, and being a superhero, a ghoul, a demon, was safer than being us, dirty kids with smudged faces in the rubble of an old building, sharing gas masks to go out and scavenge for food.

Most of us were too young to remember, but there must have been some kind of virus along with all the radioactivity, to create the monsters that lived outside the walls. Some of them were just corpses, ghouls in their own right, but we knew they couldn't really hurt us. Others were still out there, their eyes glazed over, skin gray and waxy, shuffling through the streets, eating something from a can or staring at the sun. They were probably harmless, too, but they looked like the monsters imagined during the time before, when such monsters needed to be created.

As we grew, we still scavenged for food, always bringing the gas mask, grabbing candy and canned peaches. We still craved the sweet feeling of chocolate in the back of our throats or the crunch of sour fruit candy, but we craved something else, too. Other survivors like us were older and had already discovered another rush before the bombs fell. We would trade our cans for alcohol brewed in an old bucket used for laundry, crudely grown cannabis plants from their warehouse, and something else, something white and powdery that they said used to cost more than both put together.

And there were still costumes. It must have been customary for adults to celebrate, too, because we found all kinds of things. A bright, red, flashy thing with sequins glistening in the sun, just a leotard, great for showing off legs, and a cape. A huge gorilla costume, another thing that was good for the frights we still craved. There was makeup, lipstick, wigs, even hair dye, although we wondered how safe that was.

As we grew older, we still went running through the steamy halls, hiding from each other and jumping out, but this time, we planned ahead. Those we traded with became our guests, and we flipped our mattresses across the wall and adorned the old rusty pipes with spiderwebs and sequined bats from the store. They brought the drinks and drugs, and we brought the candy, setting it out in dishes, secreting it in our pockets for later in the night. We all smelled a little sweet, and we always had candy on our breath.

I still remember the night we brought out the most candy, when the halls of our warehouse were the most full. There was someone in every corner, slumped over, drinking or smoking, laughing in clusters, or wrapped in an embrace. I danced through the halls, hiding behind every corner. I was wearing red velvet with sparkles across my face.

I first saw her sitting behind some old pipes, softly crying and eating Starbursts on the floor. She would unwrap one, look at it closely, and then nibble on it, all while tears ran down her face.

I asked her what was wrong, and she said they tasted of childhood, like memories. She said she remembered her father unwrapping them for her after a night of going door to door collecting candy when the world was safe. I closed my eyes and tried to remember my father, or my mother, or going door to door to get candy, but the only memory there was the one that was always there, a little girl alone and crying, holding a gas mask, outside the doors of the factory.

"They just remind me of filling up on candy before bed when it was cold, but maybe that's better," I told her. "Take some home with you."

When we kissed, it was like an explosion behind my eyes, like the first time someone jumped out and scared me inside the warehouse and I knew it was just for fun, the first time I ran as fast as I could and slid on the cool metal ramp that led down to the room below, the first time I tasted a Strawberry Blow Pop.

We both had glitter on our faces. When her tears were dry, we got up, and hand in hand, went to look down at the street below. The grey people shuffled past, moaning, some eating out of cans, some groaning, others too sick to walk slumped on the sidewalk. Why that wasn't us I still wasn't sure. Maybe they had purposely put the children into a place where we would be safe? Maybe we ran and hid from our families?

She stuck her hand out of the cracked window pane and tossed down the Starburst wrapper, watching it wind its way down to the ground like an autumn leaf. I pulled a handful of glitter out of my pocket and tossed it after her wrapper, watching it slowly fall against the grey-black sky.

Her eyes looked like the night sky, pink glitter set against smoky smudges made darker by tears. She was still sniffling a little, but she was also smiling.

"Let's go find some more candy."

THE VOYAGE

We spun further and further into space, rotating slowly on our ever-flowing axis. Earth became the small blue dot from the famous photographs, then a pinpoint, and then it became nothing, completely, as the endless void swallowed us up. There were five of us on the ship—myself along with Erik, Dawna, Shal, and Endina. We were selected specially because of our outstanding psych evaluations in addition to our physical fitness scores and our high marks on the entrance exam for becoming explorers. Because of the lengthy nature of our voyage, any objects that could easily be used for violence, sexual or physical, were removed.

Not only were there no pleasure sticks, there were also no brooms, no forks, no hairdryers. We were told about how in the past, people did experiments with groups in close, isolated quarters to practice for space missions, and the women were raped. As such, the Directors did everything within their power to make sure that nothing like that happened now.

The ship itself was a new prototype—a saucer based on plans that were abandoned back in the 1960s. The open floor plan made things less claustrophobic, and the ease of dropping down walls with the touch of a button allowed instant access to privacy. And the anti-gravity, the floating through space, was somehow calming.

I used my Vidlink often to listen to messages from my partner, Alena, on earth, but as we got further away from that small, blue dot, her problems also seemed smaller and smaller. I could not explain or put into words why I wasn't sympathetic about things like trouble at work or a refusal from the Birthing Center. These things should have been devastating, but I was gone by that time, shooting off into the stars, living among them and dreaming of what lay beyond that endless curtain of night.

***

It was revealed to us that we would not be returning to earth. The ship was equipped with its own small Birthing Center—a fact we knew from the beginning, but we all assumed we were going to be doing experiments there and not actually creating life. Apparently, we carried with us everything needed to set up a new society, the idea being that eventually, everyone could leave Earth behind. We were, the Vid stream we watched told us, the greatest hope for humanity's future.

Oddly, I was not angry about leaving Alena, or being ripped from my family. This was something that troubled me often. The other travelers all went through the typical stages of grief. At first they denied that anything was wrong, or happening. Then they cried, for days and days, at the loss of their families, units, and lives on Earth. Next they got angry—they threw things, broke things. Dawna even almost hit me once coming out of the shower for accidentally grabbing her towel.

After some days of storming around in anger, they all came together to hug, cry, comfort each other, and even make love. I did not participate in any of this. I never cried for Alena, and somehow, I wasn't angry. I felt, deep down, that since the moment of my birth; this was my destiny.

But it wasn't as though I didn't have any feelings. My heart broke for Alena, a thousand times. For our love for each other and the fact that we could never have a child together. And for leaving her and hurting her chance of having a normal, happy life. It was just that I felt completely at peace with my destiny. It was as though I had cancer or some other terminal disease—my heart would break, but it was the nature of my body to deteriorate before those of my loved ones, so nothing could be done.

***

When the saucer finally touched down on the surface of the planet, I was ready. I think we all were by that point, and despite the mixed emotions of the past few years, we were all prepared to embark on the next stage of our journey. It was comforting to know we had scientific work to do and things to set up, and comforting to be on solid ground, living more closely to the way we did back on Earth.

Something was puzzling me—not exactly bothering me, but puzzling me. Erik and Dawna had paired off, as had Shala and Endina. Of course there was some intermingling of sexual encounters between us, even with me at that point, but it was clear that the two groups had paired off as new life partners. I did not mind, but I didn't understand why, if this had been the intention all along, they hadn't sent six of this on the mission.

I asked Erik about this one night as we sat in the newly constructed living quarters outside the shuttle, listening to the harsh howl of Martian winds outside. With the fire indoors and the hot cocoa we were drinking, it was almost a little like being on Earth in the winter, and despite the alienness and aloneness of it all, I felt cozy and grounded. Dawna and Shal had drifted off to bed, and Endina was in the kitchen cleaning up after dinner.

"Erik," I asked, "I love that I can share this life with you all as pairs by my side. But why would they not send me someone to pair off with? Why would there not have been six of us?"

Erik laughed a little. "You mean you don't know—you haven't figured it out already?"

I shook my head.

"You had the highest marks in physical fitness and school, and the psych evals." he explained.

"You also were the first selected for the mission, and you were repeatedly denied a child on Earth despite these things and how capable you are. Didn't you think it was odd?"

"Of course, but when I was chosen for the mission I assumed that was the reason," I answered. "But are you saying—"

"Yes, you are meant to lead us," said Erik with a smile. "You are to be the Keeper here. So you will never take a mate, although you can seek pleasure with us whenever you wish. And you will have a child—you will be tasked to care for the new Keeper, your offspring, all alone."

I felt tears welling up in my eyes—I did not care about leading; all I cared about was that I would finally have a child.

"I have one more surprise for you," smiled Erik

He got up and began walking towards the wall.

"I set up the Simulator for us today, and we are running a new program. I didn't want you to be lonely, so I put in a special code for you. Now you don't have to be alone."

He pressed a button, and a blue light enveloped the room. There was a low hum, and some smoke emanated from the portal built into the wall. After it cleared, I saw Alena standing there in the smoke.

"Hello. I am here for your pleasure."

She smiled a cold smile, and the glint in her eyes reminded me of the cold, red rocks outside.

"I am here for your pleasure. How can I please you?"

Tears started to well in my eyes, and I turned furious to Erik, who seemed to mistake my anger and hurt for gratitude.

"I know she is only a sex drone, but it must be so good to see her again. You never have to be alone again Aramea—she is here to keep up company at night."

She grinned and winked a little.

"She is here to please you."

I grabbed the knife out of the hilt on my utility belt and flew at the unnatural, blue-tinted Alena. I screamed and cried and threw myself on top of her, stabbing hysterically. In my mind I saw blue stars eclipsing a red moon. I saw the tides rising and falling. I saw the face of a beautiful goddess melted, dripping in golden wax, laughing like a mad machine on repeat. Then I opened my eyes and the vision was real—blue blood was gushing from the dying drone, and morbidly, I had accidentally jammed her gear functions into a laugh track.

The mad laugh repeated over and over as the red eyes glinted.

With the laugh slowly fading as the blue blood flooded the gears of the drone, I stood up, knife still in hand, covered with the blood and organs of the machine. Erik was now cowering in fear on the sofa, and the sight of this disgusted me more than anything. The fact that he could be so coy about something and then so unable to handle my reaction was maddening.

By this time the others had woken up or emerged from their respective rooms, and it seemed they were all in a trance. None of them went to each other for comfort. They just stood in rapt terror.

"I will accept the role of Keeper," I yelled loudly, my voice shrieking, rising above my normal tones. "But this is a new era. We will have new law. If ever any of you do something like this again, it is you I will dismember, not a drone." I felt tears welling behind my eyes, but I kept my voice steady and hard. "Erik," I said quietly, "your method of gratification was very, very wrong, but your intentions were quite right. I did desire some company tonight. You will come with me to my quarters."

Shaking, Erik looked up slowly, tears running down his face.

"But you must want some time to yourself—to—to clean up, and then I can come to you," he whispered tearfully.

I felt the same glint come into my eye that I had seen in Alena's drone eyes. Perhaps she was inside me now.

"No," I said. "I'm rather fond of how the blue offsets my features."

Erik tearfully got up and followed behind me. I could see the others behind me beginning to clean up the drone corpse, and I could hear muffled tears.

SCREENS IN THE TREES

As a child, I lived in one of the tallest trees.

I could look down and see the whole village.

I could gaze upon the face of the moon.

Silver and unraveling, reaching toward the stars.

I could feel the void calling me, and I used to confuse the twinkle of nearby screens for other stars.

I wanted to reach out and touch the ones that called to me, the ones that hummed with silent insight.

One night, as my mother was sleeping, I crept to the edge of the hut built tall in the trees and looked out through the curtains.

My mother did not know it, but if you looked straight down from that point and focused your eyes, you could easily make out what was happening on the screen in the hut below.

I saw a man—a man emblazoned on the screen, locked in a loving embrace with a woman. The shape and size of their bodies shocked me, scared me. The man's skin had a silvery glint, almost mechanical. To this day, I am not sure if what I saw was illegal pornography or an illegal pleasure drone. I just remember the blue tone of his skin.

***

One day, at the treetop playground, I looked down to see all the heads of the people in my village. I counted them by twos—I was so proud that I could count by twos, and it made the counting go a lot faster. I marveled at how all the women walked in step, with baskets on their heads. They were headed to the Simulator in order to get the things their families needed. Suddenly I saw one woman running the opposite way, past the others.

She was screaming and her head was bloodied—the basket, and a blender, had been fused to her head in an accident with the Simulator. I couldn't understand what was happening then, because of course I did not know how anything worked or how things were made. I heard the little girl behind me, who was also looking down at the women, let out a giggle. We thought surely this was something that could be fixed, and we were right—the next day, the woman was rid of both the wound and the memory of the pain. Up in the trees, watching the screaming woman run by, I was so sure nothing could touch me.

ON BEHALF OF THE MOON I'M GOING TO KILL YOU

Every summer the goddess,
the Goddess Helena must be honored.
Goods must be brought to her.
And nothing is bought, sold or created.
We look to the stars and ask them a silent question.
And Helena responds with love and light.

Every winter the blood moon eclipses the sun.
And a blue coldness comes across the earth.
Snow like steel falls to the ground,
enveloping the earth in a cold, whiteblue mist.
The red of the generator lights flash off the snow like watching eyes.
The Goddess is present and here with us.

Every fall the Goddess looks to the hills.
We know where to seek sustenance and how to fill our bellies now.
We have built machines to emulate the Goddess energy.
To feed us, clothe us, and bring forth children.

We put blankets on the newborns and look to the stars.
A gray haze settles over everything on Earth.
And we watch the leaves slowly fall from the trees, never to grow
back.

Every spring, we sing our Rites to the Goddess.
We paint our faces the color of the flowers and dance and chant.
We sing mating songs, choose partners
Many hands and faces kissing, greeting, loving,
in this black void.

I know the Goddess presence is here.
She sings throughout the galaxy.
She hums in all the machines.
She is present in my quiet moments looking out at the stars.
She whispers among the red hills of Mars
and tells secrets to parallel universes.
The goddess is here, far from sunlight and human touch,
far from the trees and the greens and the soft sounds of the forest.
The goddess is under the ice of frozen mercury seas.
The goddess is present in the dark void.
The goddess knows the secrets of the universe.
The goddess can fold everything into blackness and then unfold it
again.
The goddess is present in all things.

BATHED IN BLUE LIGHT

It was the old space ghettos that would get to me on those first missions out. I would always see them looming there, jutting out from the blackness. They looked like big ships or stations, only they were anchored to the side of a dead planet, making them look more like growths or tumors than livable structures. It was hard to imagine life going on inside them, because they looked so dead, so rotting, more like something that would suck the life out of you than something that would provide shelter from space.

On one of my early runs, I had to dock in one of them and deliver supplies they had ordered, food that we had grown and cultivated. I had been briefed on how to deal with the people I would meet on these missions, but I was still nervous, since this would be my first time encountering someone out in the field.

After docking, it seemed to take forever to walk through the long, echoing corridor that connected the main bay to the rest of the building, and even longer to climb the decrepit stairs up to the door. All around was the smell of death and decay—the walls themselves looked like they were rotting and about to crumble, and I felt, or maybe imagined, that I could hear muffled screams coming from the doors in each hall. The delivery was going all the way to the top of the stairs, and I thought I would never reach the top. I was ashamed, but part of me wanted to bolt down the stairs and run back onto the spacecraft.

When I reached the top of the staircase, the door swung open, and a man's face peered out at me. Despite my training, I shrank back. The man was shorter than me; his dirty face and angry, squinting eyes made me nervous. I didn't understand how he had saved enough credits to order a shipment from us—I had expected someone cleaner, someone just living in the ghettos temporarily.

"What is it?" His voice came out as barely a croak, as though he hadn't spoken in months.

"I have your shipment of nutrient bars—and—and I just need you to sign for them; then we can bring them up."

Just then, I looked down and noticed the small shadow moving around at his feet. It took me a moment to realize that it was a very small girl, one who couldn't be any older than five.

"Get back!" he shouted and kicked at the girl, who went running back into the darkness of the apartment.

Shaking, I let him sign the paper, unsure of what to do. Part of me wanted to strike the man, to grab the girl and run. Part of me wanted to cry, and felt strangely sorry for him, and still another part wanted to shut down altogether, to stop caring about both the man and the girl, to just do my job.

When I returned to base, my supervisor told me that people living in the ghettos sometimes adopted young orphans to get a discount from us on nutrient bars. We apparently gave them a huge discount because they had children, but they treated them terribly and kept all the food for themselves. This only strengthened my resolve to do something, say something, the next time I had to make a delivery to the small old man's apartment. I was a messenger, I told myself. I could do whatever I wanted.

When I arrived at the door, the man greeted me the same way. Only a sliver of his face appeared through the crack he opened up for me, and the same awful stench emanated from the apartment. This time, he was wordless, and he took the paper and signed, but then he looked up at me.

"Do you have a med kit that I could take on credit?" he croaked. "You can add it to my next order and decrease the number of nutrient bars."

I felt a tingling behind my eyelids. It was bad enough that he wanted to scam us, and that he was using this poor young girl to do it. Now he was asking for even more, trying to push it even further for some selfish gain.

"We aren't in the habit of giving out med kits, or anything else, on credit," I snarled. "Especially not to people who are already living off of our charity."

"Please—my daughter is very sick," he said, the hardness in his eyes softening. "Without a med kit now, I don't think she will make it until your next shipment."

He seemed to be able to read disbelief on my face, so he swung the door open a bit wider, gesturing for me to come in.

Please, come in and see," he whispered. "She's very ill."

The horrible stench coming from the apartment was overwhelming, and I almost fainted. It was something like onions and tomato sauce mixed with excrement and wiring. A soft hum came from the apartment. Their screen was on, but only on the free channel setting, so a blue light bathed the living room. The young girl was indeed lying on the couch, bathed in blue light.

I walked over, and peered down at her. Her skin was red and blotchy, and her brow was covered in sweat. An odd smell like meat that was just beginning to rot came from her skin. She didn't exactly appear to be asleep—she was twitching and making small sounds under her breath—but she was not conscious and had no idea I was approaching.

I knelt over her and instinctively drew my own emergency med kit out of my jacket. Without thinking or pausing, I pulled out the syringe marked with the red X and injected it into her arm. The man ran forward, grabbing my jacket and pulling me, hard, away from the girl.

"What are you doing!" he screamed. "You'll kill her! We are nothing to you, and you'll just exterminate her!"

All the fear flooded into me as I remembered my training. How could I have been so stupid? I had entered his apartment. I had heard everything about how those who lived in the ghettos were cunning, how they would pretend, how they possessed an inhuman amount of strength. And now he would do me in, here in his own apartment.

But he was crying—sitting on the floor with his head in his hands, sobbing, rocking back and forth. I took a good look at him for the first time. His dirty slacks didn't reach his heels, and one of his socks had a giant hole in it, so big that most of the toes on his right foot were exposed. He was balding with thin gray hair that hung like wispy wires all around his head. He was shaking, and he smelled awful. But he didn't seem evil or cunning, and I truly believed that he didn't want to hurt or kill me—he just didn't understand what I had done to his daughter.

"You don't care about us, and you're just going to kill her, dump her, because she has the plague," he muttered. "She's not even a person to you. She's not even anything."

"Tenant, there is no such thing as the plague," I responded. "She simply had scarlet fever. I carry a vaccination for it at all times; that was all she needed."

As if to prove my words, the girl had sat up. The syringe had fallen out of her arm, and she looked a bit dazed, but her skin was no longer red and flushed, and she wasn't sweating.

The man ran over, picked her up, and held her close to his chest. She began to cry, rubbing her arm over her father's shoulder where the needle had pricked.

I knelt next to them, still keeping my distance from the man, but looking the little girl in the eyes.

"Yes, that's a nasty shot," I told her, "but now you're all better, and before you were very sick. Your arm might be sore for a few days, but it's much, much better than being really sick."

She looked confused. "I don't remember being sick."

As though the whole thing had started to bore her, the girl pulled away from her father's grasp and walked towards the eerie, blue glow of the screen. She pressed a few buttons, and suddenly, the blue dissipated and a series of colorful bunnies danced in their place. There was music on in the background, and she contentedly walked back a few steps and planted herself in a cross-legged position on the floor in front of the TV.

The father looked up from his place on the floor, where he had remained after the girl walked away. The look in his eyes was pure gratitude, and for the first time, I didn't feel any kind of fear. He wouldn't hurt me now.

"Thank you," he said. "Her mother is gone. She left me years ago with her daughter."

I raised my eyebrows, slightly skeptical again. "Why would a woman abandon her own daughter?"

"Because," the man whispered, as though trying not to be heard by his daughter. "She was conceived here, in this apartment. We didn't go to a Station."

I barely understood what he meant—conceived in the apartment? But how? They barely had any equipment for basic living needs, let alone in-home reproduction.

He held my gaze and widened his eyes, and suddenly I understood what he meant. Sex between this man and some woman now living who knows where in the galaxy is what caused this girl to be here now. His sexual organ was inside the woman, and after some sort of lovemaking, she was conceived. I had studied it in history and science classes, but it hardly seemed believable that someone in this day and age could be practicing such ancient reproductive processes.

"But how—you couldn't have known what the sex would be, or her personality, eye color—" suddenly I cut off, because his eyes were still as wide as saucers. I remembered from school that sometimes men and women had sex just for pleasure, the way we all did, and accidently created a child. Clearly, the man didn't want his daughter to know that she hadn't been a planned child. I chanced a look over my shoulder at her, but she continued to be entranced by the bunnies dancing on the screen.

I stood up and pulled out the contents of my jacket. I was carrying three nutrient bars—not fare that Messengers would normally eat, but good food for being in space and unable to cook. I also had the rest of my med kit, which contained another vaccine for Scarlet Fever, and some basic bandages and disinfectants. And lastly, I held a Pleasure Capsule, which I tucked back into my jacket in a hurry, embarrassed, but I didn't think he had time to see.

"Here, take this for her," I told him. "This vaccine will do the same thing, in case you caught it or she gets it again. Clean where I gave her the shot and any other cuts, and then bandage them up.

Dirty cuts are how the fever spreads. And she'll be very hungry in an hour or so since she didn't eat during the fever—use the extra bars for that, so she won't have to go hungry later."

Before he could say anything else to me, I walked across the living room, closed the door behind me, and started down the steps. I didn't want to worry about how I would explain an entire missing med kit back at Base, but I didn't think about that. I also didn't think about what would happen if I had caught the fever and didn't have a vaccine. I just walked down the steps as quickly as I could, eager to get back on the ship.

ROSE GARDEN

Crimsons and dark purples spread out underneath the artificial, blood-red sky.

Coming here at dusk, with the world outside turning blueblack, to see all the roses in bloom, the sky always that perfect red color, reflecting, refracting the color of the roses, and multiplying.

Shivering one night, the world outside so cold, I stepped inside and breathed deeply—rose smell washing over me, all the colors lighting up so warm.

Winding my way around, down the rows and rows of endless reds, I heard a soft moan coming from the other side of the rose garden. I breathed in, but something seemed to pull me on.

There, behind the loveliest and tallest row of flowers lay a woman, skin as white as snow, with roses vivid as fresh-picked strawberries looming over her, reflecting, turning the once white-hued skin a blush of bright red.

Her soft arms were covered in blueblack bruises, and her breath came in gasps. Her eyes fluttered and she smelled of rose perfume.

On the ground next to her lay a syringe filled with blush red and a crimson black. The colors swirled together in an endless dance that was like the rose garden, tricking night into thinking it was day forever.

I stared at it. I wanted to touch it, to pick it up, to hold it, but I was afraid.

I leaned forward, barely daring to breathe, and brushed the hair from the sleeping girl's eyes. Her breath came in a few soft gasps, as if sensing the touch, and then she shifted a little. I drew back, afraid I woke her.

The gasps of breath stopped, and the girl lay still. I leaned over once more, mesmerized. Her eyelids no longer fluttered, and her chest no longer heaved. All was still, except the almost indiscernible hum of the red, red roses closing in. The room seemed to reflect an even deeper color than before.

I stepped back.

Her face had changed—suddenly I no longer saw a sleeping, beautiful girl, a girl who looked like she was receiving intense pleasure. I saw a ghost, a corpse, an aged and bitter woman. I turned to run.

Later I learned it was Retina, the extract of poppies, and the red, red glow I craved was not a rose garden, but a poppy garden, grown so we could cultivate Retina. No matter how hard we tried to deny it, there were addicts of Retina, even here. They snuck into the poppy room to use in private, to enhance the effects of the poison, even to try and steal the poppies if they became desperate.

It occurred to me that I may have found the rose garden so comforting, despite the garish red hue, because of the poppies, and that scared me.

I didn't like the idea of something else coming into my brain, working the wires, making me feel things. I heard about the death, and I learned about Retina, but I never told anyone what I saw, and I never returned to the rose garden again. Its beauty was permanently marred, and I even crossed the street when I saw the red dome looming, and smelled the sickly red smell on the air.

FIRST MISSION

The first time I spun out into space for more than just a simple day mission, I was 21 years old. I wasn't used to being away from everyone. I wasn't used to being outside of gravity for days at a time, outside of myself. But, in a strange way, I liked how the days and nights folded into each other. I welcomed the feeling of not knowing night from day, not caring, not wanting to know. It wasn't that I was depressed or didn't miss the sunlight, but it was comforting to think that in some ways, a world without all the people I held dear wasn't like the normal world. It was suspended, outside of time.

I was assigned to room with Tala, a loud, bubbly, outgoing girl from a nearby station. This was also her first mission, and unlike me, she seemed to be dealing with her nerves by never shutting her mouth. She had bright red hair and a streak of blood-red freckles across her nose, and seemed to talk of nothing other than home, when I was trying so desperately to forget.

"I got a vid from Nik today," she chirped, plopping down on her bunk.

I briefly looked up from my book, wishing hard that she wouldn't give me every detail of the vid, but my lack of response didn't stop her from plunging into a monologue.

"Of course, it was an old vid, a month old, because of the time difference, but he has such attention to detail. He was asking me about today, instead of last month. Have I already mentioned he is getting his Law Certificate?"

I struggled not to roll my eyes. She had only mentioned it about a thousand times. I felt I knew Nik's academic history almost better than my own by this point.

"Of course I did! Silly me; I do go on about him, but cross my stars if he isn't the most handsome man at Base! Anyway, do you know what he said? He said that if he gets his certificate and passes, he is going to put in for a shuttle to meet me!"

She actually squealed.

"Isn't that fantastic? I could be holed-up in a bubble bath before I even get home! Wow, I miss bubble baths. Oh, and I do miss the food! At your station, do you all have the little cakes, the yellow ones with the pink frosting? Oh of course you do, we must get the same food rations, you're so close..."

I looked back down at my book, hoping she'd take the hint, but she kept droning on in the background. I focused hard, not wanting her to see the tears in my eyes, thinking of home, of Mala and how she wanted me to quit the explorer program.

***

The next day in the dining hall, I took a seat as far from the others as possible, hoping to be left alone with my book, not much wanting to chat about the lovers we had left behind, our lives at our stations or on Base. In the back of my mind, I kept imagining the shuttle exploding into a million pieces. It wasn't that I was afraid to be in space—this was what I thrived on—and it wasn't like there had been an accident at all in the past hundred years. It just felt like everything around me was going to collapse at any minute.

"Can I sit here?"

I looked up to see a woman so beautiful I almost felt pain in the back of my eyes. Her long, black hair looked almost blue in the glaring, fluorescent lights of the dining hall, and her small, green eyes flickered over me, as if she already knew everything about me that she needed to and had somehow decided I was the best choice to sit next to in the hall, given her limited options. Her high cheekbones and pale skin almost seemed to glow, and even though she was wearing the same Explorer outfit as everyone else, its unsightly, gray bulges couldn't hide her curves.

"We don't have to talk—I just don't want to get stuck sitting with the ones who talk on and on about their partners at home, their kids, what kind of food they are going to eat when they get home—it's all so dull. For Neptune's sake, we are all finally out in the middle of the stars, what we've been working towards our whole lives, and they are going to sit there and whine about not getting to eat a couple of yellow cakes."

She flashed me a devilish smile, swung a boot around the side of the seat, and plopped down hard. It occurred to me for a split second that I hadn't actually told her it was OK to sit down, but I was a little intrigued now, and couldn't seem to stop staring at her long hair and flashing, green eyes.

"Have you met Tala, then?" I asked, chuckling a little in spite of myself.

"Oh yes, she's my training mate for parachute deployment," she groaned. "I practically know her family history. I certainly know her dietary history, and everything about that husband of hers. You'd think all these people are the first to have made love, or to have tasted food."

"Tell me about it—she's my bunkmate." I spoke up despite my desire to keep my head down and keep reading my book. I didn't need a friend. But something about this woman... It occurred to me that I still didn't even know her name.

"Your bunkmate?" She leaned forward and stared me directly in the eyes, barely blinking. "No wonder you are sitting over here by yourself—you must not get a moment of peace in your bunk. In that case, I'm sorry to have imposed in the first place."

"It's OK. It's—nice to talk to someone who isn't just talking about cake," I trailed off lamely. I actually was starting to enjoy myself, in spite of my initial misgivings. This was the first conversation I had had that wasn't just about Base, and it was refreshing.

She cut off my train of thought, laughing. "Good to know—I'm Lasha."

"So," she continued, "you don't have anyone back on Base to talk about?"

"Oh no—I do, have someone—a woman."

"Oh," she raised her eyebrows and looked at me meaningfully. "So, we play for the same team?

"Don't almost all the women who sign up for duty?" I laughed. "But yeah, we are gonna make it official when I get back. She's great, it's just..."

I suddenly found myself unable to be as well-spoken as I normally was, under the oddly pleasant icy stare of Lasha.

"I miss her, and it's easier to not think about her all the time; it keeps me from getting homesick. Besides, like you said, we are out here in the stars, and I guess I'm just trying to make the most of it."

After that, we talked for hours, whiling away the rest of the afternoon free time, which I had intended to spend reading. We didn't talk about Base or people back home again, but we spent a lot of time discussing our trajectory, the work we would do harvesting from the star once we arrived, our earliest memories of watching broadcasts of space missions, and our school days, studying everything we could about space. Like me, Lasha not only excelled in physical fitness and math and science, like most of the explorers, but also in the humanities and literature, which was rare, because anyone good in those subjects tended to study law and stay out of the stars.

Over the next few days, we spent more and more time together, walking and talking together during every break, and sitting together during every meal. Each time, we purposely avoided the topics of Base and our lives at home. All I managed to glean about Lasha that didn't have to do with exploration, the mission, or academics was that she did not have a love interest or children, and that she was living on Base with an aunt to save up for her own place. I didn't pry about the lack of love interest, or the fact that she wasn't self-sufficient enough to live alone and lived with an aunt rather than a parent.

Like the lack of night and day, it seemed that Lasha and I existed in a place outside of real time.

***

I never planned to go to bed with Lasha, but one night it happened. I think the others all thought it was happening long before it was. They all whispered behind their hands as we walked by, but I had already decided that my relationship with Lasha was purely professional and was actually very beneficial to my career.

While the rest of the women were idly gossiping about what they would do and eat when they got back home, what they missed, and their wives and lovers, Lasha and I were talking star trajectories and what missions we should take on next. I reasoned that talking to Lasha was just as good as spending all my time reading and studying, because our conversations were so enriching mentally. In fact, rather than sitting in the port bar late into the night and drinking with the rest of the team, we would retire early to read and learn so that we would have more to talk about the next day.

But one day, Lasha proudly pulled out a bottle of blackberry vodka from under the table at lunch. The drink was so bluepurple in color that it looked almost like her hair, and it glinted beautifully, even under the florescent lights.

"I thought tonight we could blow off some steam," she told me. "We dock tomorrow morning, so this will be the last night of our first mission."

I wracked my brain, trying to think of a reason not to indulge with Lasha.

"Don't you think we should be rested then—for the landing, I mean? We don't want to make any mistakes."

Lasha laughed and shook her shiny hair off of her forehead, eyes dancing. "Please, we are by far the best prepared for this mission—it's all we've been talking about, while everyone else has been gossiping. We are going to make the best impression by far, no matter if we drink or not."

Her smile was so contagious that I couldn't help but smile back and nod, hoping maybe she would fall asleep, or forget to send me a vid message.

But directly after lights out, I received a buzz on my vidlink, and Lasha's smiling face appeared.

"Come over and have a drink with me," she said enthusiastically.

I could see from the screen that she was sitting on her bed, wearing nothing but a blood-red silk robe that offset the intense shades of her hair.

I arrived at her door, and was surprised to find a lack of bunkmate when I entered. "Where is Salana?" I asked. Her bunkmate was known for being incredibly punctual and sleeping as many hours as she could, so it was uncharacteristic of her not to already be tucked in bed.

"She went to the deck to watch the docking," she told me. "Haven't you heard—rumor is we are running ahead of schedule. The dying star should be visible in about two hours, and we will be docking nearby. So we won't be at a disadvantage at all—everyone will be up half the night trying to catch the first glimpse of that star."

We talked for what felt like days, the blackberry liquor slowly making my limbs feel heavy, my mind feel numb. After a while, I felt as though I was lost at sea, awash in Lasha's long, luxurious black hair. I realized that a strand of it had fallen onto my shoulder, we were sitting so close together. I could feel her breath on my neck, and I could tell from the feeling creeping up from my toes that my face was flushing as bright red as her robe.

When we finally made love, it was all swishes and motion, dark colors and smooth silk. Her pale white skin contrasted so starkly with the red of her robe and the black of her hair that I began to see nothing but a purplish swirl before my eyes. The color from the drink had stained her lips a dark crimson, as though she were wearing expensive lipstick saved for special occasions. I realized at one point, with a pang of guilt, that this wasn't like any lovemaking I had ever experienced.

It was not as though my partner and I had any illusions about saving ourselves sexually for each other. We had both experimented plenty in our younger days, and just as she didn't expect me to remain faithful for months on end in space, I would hardly be upset if she spent a night making love with one of our friends on Base.

But the intensity, the power, and the way our bodies melded and flowed together, was not anything I had ever experienced with the safe and predictable partners I'd had before.

Once the passion had subsided, we lay together on her small bunk, my head awkwardly fitting into the crook of her arm. She had both arms up beside her head, as though she were cradling it, and she looked more regal and majestic than ever, like someone caught in the middle of dancing or posing for a painting. Suddenly, the light in the room changed, and instead of being bathed in dim, fluorescent lighting only, Lasha's face seemed to glow bright red, matching the tone of her pale skin to that of her vibrant robe.

With a gasp, Lasha popped up in bed and leaned over me, craning her graceful neck as far as it would go. I slid out from under her and put my feet on the floor, shakily standing up.

"Earmos—the dead star," she breathed. It sounded like a curse or a spell—like the start of a poem. I suddenly wanted her to say more about the star, even though we had already poured over its every detail, its diameter, how far from it we would need to dock, and the process for harvesting energy from the star as it expelled its last throes out into the local solar system.

The ship had shifted from the impossibly fast slowness of light speed, where all was black and gray, to a slow crawl, bringing the endless night back into focus. In the distance beyond the star, I could see the docking station—a small outcropping, not too different from the space ghettos back home, where we would make our home base.

Although I knew like the back of my hand that this solar system had been dead for millions of years longer than ours had existed, that if there had ever been life here, it was long, long, long, long gone, I couldn't help but shiver as I imagined the dead planet had once been as alive and green and vibrant as the tree villages on Base, that the star has once shone with as much brilliance as our sun.

I knew that in all likelihood, the planets in this solar system were either too tightly packed near the star, or too far away, for life to have evolved, but in my mind, gray, dusty phantoms of the dead world danced around the ship, pulling us closer to their dead world, begging us to come free them from the confines of their dying star.

Lasha's cold but somehow comforting hand on my shoulder softly pulled me out of my dramatic revere.

"I never knew something dying could be so beautiful," she breathed. "It's dying, but it is giving its life to us now—even knowing all the science behind it, all the technicalities of how it works, how we ourselves are going to do it, there is still something so beautiful, so poetic about that."

"Death is always a beautiful process because of the way it gives back, but it doesn't always look this blatantly beautiful," I murmured.

Lasha took my hand and softly smiled, looking from me to the dying star. "Would you like to go up to the deck and join the others?"

We polished off the remaining blackberry drink, and, hand-in-hand, walked through the hall and took the lift up to the main deck of the ship. Normally, our gossipy crew mates wouldn't have been able to stop whispering about how we were together, but the dead star seemed to have cast a somber spell on our crew. The monotony of deep space travel and close quarters rumors didn't seem to apply anymore in the light of the mysterious apparition.

The ship's lights had been dimmed to better view the star, and most of the women on board had their vid lights on, so that they could still see each other or read data about the star. The effect, though unintentional, reminded me of the candles back on Luna for the death ceremony of the New Moon. It was as though we were holding a vigil for the dying star, paying our quiet respects before we crept in and stole its last energy.

Lasha softly let go of my hand, and slipped her arm around my shoulders, holding me close while we looked at the dead star before us in the endless black sky.

DEPARTURE

May the goddesses part and welcome
our sister back into the earth, back into the heavens.
May her face ever reflect the kindness of the clouds.
May her daughters ever look to the moon and see her face.
Aha-mea dea dis faeraha
May the goddess bless her, may the goddess absorb her.
May the moons forever shine with her in the sky.
May the New Moon be banished forever, into eternal darkness.
Aha-mea dea dis faeraha

THE CEREMONY

I didn't want to become a woman. To have to iron, clean my dresses, give up my dolls, start looking for someone to court. I didn't feel like doing any of those things, but I thought that when I first bled, somehow I'd suddenly want all of it.

"This part of the Ceremony is secret," whispered Elize, the Ceremony Director, when I met her at the end of a long, blue hallway filled with the sound of a thousand voices.

I knew that I was about to be privy to something only the women had seen. Not the girls, the women. I felt a dampness between my legs that meant it was already time to change the garment. No one had told me that the blood actually came out like bleeding, like a wound. Or maybe, I wondered, the fear and excitement make it come out more. Maybe this is part of The Ceremony.

I pushed open the door before me, and screamed.

The walls were smeared with blood. The stench was awful, but the images on the walls were worse. Women being burned alive in front of laughing men and women. Women having their privates cut. I squirmed and turned away.

"These are our mothers, and this is in memory of what they had to suffer," said Elize. "We come here to remember, to let their pain become our pain. Use your blood, take your rag, and wipe it on the wall as a sign that you understand."

To the shame of my foremothers, I didn't complete the ritual. I couldn't breathe. I swayed, losing balance, losing sense. I fell to the ground before Elize could catch me. The other women gossiped that Elize didn't like children—why she did the Ceremonies, and it showed on her face. Clearly I was still a child, not ready to be wise to the ways of the old world and accept that we can save ourselves through some ritual act.

HE

She spun her way through city streets and never once lost sight of him. He was her guide, and her way through. He protected her when no one else would, fiercely, with an irreplaceable love and assurance.

He put a mask on her face and led her through the underground tunnels, past those she shouldn't look at, past the chemical fires and the final sunsets and the dead or dying bodies. They held each other when the bombs went off and they crawled under buildings when they had to avoid a roving gang.

They even made love. Once, although it was only once after finding a bottle of wine under a bridge. She knew he watched her as she slept, and tried to keep her from harm. But still, she saw the way he drank too much and snapped at the sleeping men they passed in the alleys, and the way he lied and cheated when he didn't really have to.

One night, they were sleeping in an old, abandoned hotel shaded by palm trees and overlooking the pool. They watched the stars blink out, one by one. Then, a man came to their room, pinned him against the wall, and stabbed him to death. She didn't know whether he owed the man money, whether he was involved with the man, or if it was a random incident. She thought he would come for her next, and she flattened herself into the corner. But he looked right at her, his eyes a painful, piercing red, and then left.

She cried, and she mourned him, and she lay beside his body for a while. She thought about all the times they laid together, all the times they wove through the streets together. She thought of the back of his head, his long, blond, curly hair the only thing visible through her mask. She thought about the groping fingers, always feeling for her, and his hands always keeping her out of reach. Then, she got up, walked out, and headed for the door.

DRIFT

As she opened the hatch and slid out into the starry night, she heard a scraping sound behind her. She didn't have to turn around to know who it was.

Marika had been avoiding Dante the entire time on the ship. Ever since their breathless encounter in the elevator, the one Marika had pulled away from, Dante seemed to be stalking her around every corner. At night, she locked her door, waiting as quietly as possible until she heard his footsteps fade down the hall and disappear. She was constantly running.

But now, here in "the library," their term for the spiraling vortex of levers that controlled the fuel tanks, there was nowhere to go, and Dante knew it.

He moved toward her, eyes flashing, and grabbed her arm. Even in her spacesuit, Marika felt he was seeing straight through to her naked body, then to her bones. She kicked herself away from the wall of the ship, her cord holding. Dante kicked off too, floating toward her, then grabbed both her arms and pinned them to her sides.

Using all her force, Marika spun around and kicked hard, sending him flying further from the ship.

The tether broke. Immediately, the fear in his eyes turned to hopeless panic. He began waving his arms wildly, and then he started drifting soundlessly into space.

Calmly, Marika turned around and began her work on the controls. She ignored his silent screams, trapped in a pink bubble in the nebula they were floating in. She didn't turn around to see his eyes begin to turn red or his veins bulge out, and she kept her gaze averted from the carnage that became his face as he died in space, just a few feet from their vessel.

She finished her work calmly, then floated over to his body and gave it a hard kick. It started to drift away. Her tether was extended all the way, and for a moment, she thought of following him, letting her body drift soundlessly after his into the ether.

Then she slowly kicked off his body and propelled herself back into the ship. She landed soundlessly, crawled along the hull, and reached over to open the hatch.

VIRUS 08394

The virus had started slowly. No one really noticed it at first. Waking up from deep space hibernation often had side effects like nausea, fatigue, and even a light fever. And these particular travelers had been asleep for hundreds of years.

They were now only a few light years away from a planet they knew contained life. They were about to make the biggest discovery in the history of mankind, but they were dying slowly.

The first woman to exhibit symptoms was quarantined in a small, dark room. Even the light made her skin peel. She was violently ill, unable to eat, sleep, or hear. She could still see, but everything took on an eerie hue.

One by one, this happened to all of them. Attempts were made to contact Earth, to change course, to even reenter hibernation. But it was as if even the ship was sick. None of the systems were working, and slowly, it became evident that oxygen was in short supply.

They probably had about three days left. Panic set in, with the men tearing out each other's throats and feasting on them, the women systematically removing each other's ears with forks in sick bay. Two women collided in the hall outside the bathroom and began clawing each other fiercely, blood and flesh flying, until they both collapsed in a bloody pulp.

Eventually, when only a few remained, a message flashed onto all the view screens in the ship. It started with a red flower blooming, then showed white text both in an alien language and, to their surprise, plain English.

"Virus 08304 protocol Rose" has run its course. All systems that have been experiencing malfunction will shortly terminate.

Termination estimate: 3 hours Earth TIME

Reason for termination: detection of Planet E0475320

Before the few bloodied survivors had time to react, the ship blinked, glowed red, and then exploded into a billion pieces. Each atom exploded into particles smaller than those known to man. Unlike an atomic explosion, there was no sound, no cloud, no radiation. There was simply nothing left.

The virus had run is course. Only the hologram of a bright, red flower hung in its place.

GOLD SKY DEATH BLOOM

The sky was golden and everything was ending. The world was slowly burning up before our very eyes. Mothers clung to children as they vaporized, or turned a chilling golden gray before sweltering and becoming ash.

It was hot, too hot, and there were too many viruses and contagions to be anywhere without a life support suit. Plus there was all the radiation. But there was a shortage of suits. There was a shortage of everything, although there was a rumor that the gold, protective suits hung there, behind glass, swinging, waiting for someone rich enough to use them.

So we stayed in our little hovel, our hut, our house, and we clung to each other. Strangers. We clung and we cried and we gasped for air. Sometimes the sunlight crested golden and peaked through the window, a little tendril of radiation; a little ray of death. We welcomed night now, when we could push our faces up by the window in the sickly-soft moon glow and whisper "I remember."

Everything was dulled by an eerie, gray light, the opposite of gold, and a cold silence crept through the moonlight, but at least you could breathe easier.

Then dawn came, and more corpses, pulled from their homes, littering the ground, no more protective suits, only gold-gray ash spreading everywhere.

When they came for us, we were screaming, clawing, twisting, fighting, our way out, burning into the golden sun, blood vessels bursting, our bodies glowing red from the radiation. This is how it feels, I thought, this is how it feels to be blistering, to be raw, to have absolutely no shelter, then all was white hot screams and clawing, and then all was cool and black, a long burst... and then dark and cool.

Surrounded by a moonglow, I floated on into nothingness. Angelic, silver, weightless.

RESPIRATOR III

When she could go no further, Neeka collapsed by the side of the road. She barely had time to roll off the path into the ditch before sleep totally overtook her.

The next day, she began to walk in the direction of the rising smoke again. She knew a lot of the other cities out there were a lot worse off, but she also knew there were other people out there. She just had to keep following the smoke.

On the third day, Neeka was beyond exhaustion. She had eaten nothing but a can of beans from an abandoned gas station food mart and was about to pass out. Her feet were bloody, bruised, and cracked, and she was caked with dirt from the dry, dusty wind, and from sleeping beside the road.

Up ahead of her, the highway ended. The bridge she was walking across ended abruptly, guardrails dangling over the world below.

Breaking almost into a run, Neeka covered the rest of the distance before the road was cut off. She looked down at the dizzying sight below.

Down in the burned-out city, she could see a few lanes of traffic moving, some back-and-forth on the highway and in parking lots. So it wasn't abandoned. It was alive. It was even somewhat safe.

Close to the edge of the city, she saw what looked like a park. It was full of people. They had gathered together. Some were singing, some were drinking and sharing food. Even from where she sat, she could hear laughter, talking. Suddenly a sound rose above the crowd, and she recognized the song, one she had heard before.

This land was made for you and me...

Acknowledgements

Thanks to all the writers who have inspired me, Harlan Ellison, Margaret Atwood, Doris Lessing, Ray Bradbury, Mick Farren, and more. Thank you to Spaceboy for taking a chance on this book, publishing me, and keeping science fiction alive!

Thanks to *Suspect Press*, *Birdy*, and *South Broadway Ghost Society* for regularly publishing my work and encouraging me. Thanks to Amanda E.K. for making time to teach and mentor me, and for my mom for introducing me to writing and reading so early on.

Thanks to my dad for supporting all my weird hobbies, and to the entire *OUT FRONT* team for being my family. Thanks to New Noise and Lisa Root for making my music writing dreams come true.

And most of all, thanks to Wil Wilson and Lexi Holtzer for always being there for me and supporting me.

About the Author

Addison Herron-Wheeler is editor at *OUT FRONT* Magazine, web editor at *New Noise* Magazine, and the author of *Wicked Woman: Women in Metal from 1969 to Now*. She's an extreme introvert, avid metal-listener and sci-fi-reader, and human rights advocate.

About the Publishing Team

Nate Ragolia was labeled as "weird" early in elementary school, and it stuck. He's a lifelong lover of science fiction, and a nerd/geek. In 2015 his first book, *There You Feel Free,* was published by 1888's Black Hill Press. He's also the author of *The Retroactivist*, published by Spaceboy Books. He founded and edits BONED, an online literary magazine, has created webcomics, and writes whenever he's not playing video games or petting dogs.

Shaunn Grulkowski has been compared to Warren Ellis and Phillip K. Dick and was once described as what a baby conceived by Kurt Vonnegut and Margaret Atwood would turn out to be. He's at least the fifth best Slavic-Latino-American sci-fi writer in the Baltimore metro area. He's the author of *Retcontinuum,* and the editor of *A Stalled Ox* and *The Goldfish,* among others.